SandCastle™

Homophones

Sue Threw the Goop Through the Hoop

Amanda Rondeau

ABDO
Publishing Company

Published by SandCastle™, an imprint of ABDO Publishing Company, 4940 Viking Drive, Edina, Minnesota 55435.

Cover and interior photo credits: Corbis Images, Digital Stock, Digital Vision, Eyewire Images, PhotoDisc

Library of Congress Cataloging-in-Publication Data

Rondeau, Amanda, 1974-
   Sue threw the goop through the hoop / Amanda Rondeau.
      p. cm. -- (Homophones)
   Includes index.
   Summary: Photographs and simple text introduce homophones, words that sound alike but are spelled differently and have different meanings.
   ISBN 1-57765-783-7 (hardcover)
   ISBN 1-59197-073-3 (paperback)
   1. English language--Homonyms--Juvenile literature. [1. English language--Homonyms.] I. Title. II. Series.

PE1595 .R73 2002
428.1--dc21

2001053371

The SandCastle concept, content, and reading method have been reviewed and approved by a national advisory board including literacy specialists, librarians, elementary school teachers, early childhood education professionals, and parents.

Let Us Know

After reading the book, SandCastle would like you to tell us your stories about reading. What is your favorite page? Was there something hard that you needed help with? Share the ups and downs of learning to read. We want to hear from you! To get posted on the ABDO Publishing Company Web site, send us email at:

sandcastle@abdopub.com

About SandCastle™

A professional team of educators, reading specialists, and content developers created the SandCastle™ series to support young readers as they develop reading skills and strategies and increase their general knowledge. The SandCastle™ series has four levels that correspond to early literacy development in young children. The levels are provided to help teachers and parents select the appropriate books for young readers.

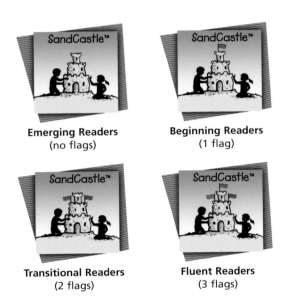

Emerging Readers
(no flags)

Beginning Readers
(1 flag)

Transitional Readers
(2 flags)

Fluent Readers
(3 flags)

These levels are meant only as a guide. All levels are subject to change.

ABDO
Publishing Company

To see a complete list of SandCastle™ books and other nonfiction titles from ABDO Publishing Company, visit www.abdopub.com or contact us at:
4940 Viking Drive, Edina, Minnesota 55435 • 1-800-800-1312 • fax: 1-952-831-1632

thyme   time

Homophones are words that sound alike but are spelled differently and have different meanings.

Sam is looking for a great tale.

This elephant has a long tail.

Stephanie is sad.

She has tears in her eyes.

This cake has three tiers.

We have to pay tax when we buy a car.

These tacks mark places on
a map.

A queen sits on a throne.

The ball was thrown to Tim.

He caught it.

We go for walks at low tide.

Haley tied her shoes all by herself.

Ben tows a van that needs to be fixed.

Our toes touch the sand.

A tee is used to hold a golf ball.

Some people drink hot tea in the afternoon.

Marcus is being towed **by the boat.**

What is Brian holding?

(a toad)

Words I Can Read

Nouns

A noun is a person, place, or thing

afternoon (af-tur-NOON) p. 19
ball (BAWL) p. 13
boat (BOTE) p. 20
cake (KAYK) p. 9
car (KAR) p. 10
elephant (EL-uh-fuhnt) p. 7

golf ball (GOLF BAWL) p. 18
map (MAP) p. 11
queen (KWEEN) p. 12
sand (SAND) p. 17
tail (TAYL) p. 7
tale (TAYL) p. 6
tax (TAKS) p. 10
tea (TEE) p. 19

tee (TEE) p. 18
throne (THROHN) p. 12
thyme (TIME) p. 4
tide (TIDE) p. 14
time (TIME) p. 4
toad (TOHD) p. 21
van (VAN) p. 16

Plural Nouns

A plural noun is more than one person, place, or thing

eyes (EYEZ) p. 8
homophones (HOME-uh-fonez) p. 5
meanings (MEE-ningz) p. 5

people (PEE-puhl) p. 19
places (PLAYSS-ez) p. 11
shoes (SHOOZ) p. 15
tacks (TAKSS) p. 11

tears (TIHRZ) p. 8
tiers (TIHRZ) p. 9
toes (TOHZ) p. 17
walks (WAWKSS) p. 14
words (WURDZ) p. 5

Proper Nouns

A proper noun is the name of a person, place, or thing

Ben (BEN) p. 16
Brian (BRYE-uhn) p. 21
Haley (HAY-lee) p. 15

Marcus (MAR-kuhss) p. 20
Sam (SAM) p. 6

Stephanie (STEF-a-nee) p. 8
Tim (TIM) p. 13

Verbs

A verb is an action or being word

are (AR) p. 5
be (BEE) p. 16
being (BEE-ing) p. 20
buy (BYE) p. 10
caught (KAWT) p. 13
drink (DRINGK) p. 19
fixed (FIKST) p. 16
go (GOH) p. 14
has (HAZ) pp. 7, 8, 9
have (HAV) pp. 5, 10

hold (HOHLD) p. 18
holding (HOHLD-ing) p. 21
is (IZ) pp. 6, 8, 18, 20, 21
looking (LUK-ing) p. 6
mark (MARK) p. 11
needs (NEEDZ) p. 16
pay (PAY) p. 10
sits (SITSS) p. 12

sound (SOUND) p. 5
spelled (SPELD) p. 5
thrown (THROHN) p. 13
tied (TIDE) p. 15
touch (TUHCH) p. 17
towed (TOHD) p. 20
tows (TOHZ) p. 16
used (YOOZD) p. 18
was (WUHZ) p. 13

Adjectives

An adjective describes something

alike (uh-LIKE) p. 5
different (DIF-ur-uhnt) p. 5
great (GRAYT) p. 6
her (HUR) pp. 8, 15

hot (HOT) p. 19
long (LAWNG) p. 7
low (LOH) p. 14
our (OUR) p. 17
sad (SAD) p. 8

some (SUHM) p. 19
these (THEEZ) p. 11
this (THISS) pp. 7, 9
three (THREE) p. 9

Match these homophones
to the pictures

tea
tee

tears
tiers

throne
thrown

tide
tied